Splash
the
Dolphin

The Animal Friends Books

Splash
the
Dolphin

by
Cynthia Overbeck

CAROLRHODA BOOKS
MINNEAPOLIS, MINNESOTA U.S.A.

Revised English text by Cynthia Overbeck. Original French
text by Jean Saint Gem. Translation by Dyan Hammarberg.
Photographs taken at Marineland D'Antibes by J. Dumont,
J. Dupont, P. Leclerc, P. Wyns, and Explorer. Drawings
by L'Enc Matte.

LIBRARY OF CONGRESS CATALOGING IN PUBLICATION DATA

Overbeck, Cynthia.
  Splash the dolphin.

  (The Animal Friends Books)
  Original ed. published under title: Splash le dauphin.
  SUMMARY: Two youngsters visit Marine Land, where they
learn that dolphins are intelligent and friendly creatures.

  1. Dolphins—Juvenile literature. [1. Dolphins] I. Saint Gem,
Jean. Splash le dauphin. II. Dumont, J. III. Matte, L'Enc.
IV. Title.

  QL795.D709 1976   599'.53   76-1218
  ISBN 0-87614-061-4

First published in the United States of America 1976 by
Carolrhoda Books, Inc. All English language rights reserved.

Original edition published by Librairie A. Hatier, Paris,
France, under the title SPLASH LE DAUPHIN.
English text and drawings © 1976 Carolrhoda Books, Inc.
Photographs © 1973 Librairie A. Hatier.

Manufactured in the United States of America.
Published simultaneously in Canada by J. M. Dent & Sons
(Canada) Ltd., Don Mills, Ontario.

International Standard Book Number: 0-87614-061-4
Library of Congress Catalog Card Number: 76-1218

2   3   4   5   6   7   8   9   10   85   84   83   82   81   80   79   78

This is an exciting weekend for Jean and her brother, Ricky, because they are taking their first trip to Marine Land. Marine Land is a special kind of zoo where fish and other sea creatures live in huge salt-water tanks. Through glass windows in the sides of the tanks, Ricky and Jean can see all sorts of fascinating creatures—sting rays, fish, eels, and even giant sea turtles. As the children are looking through the window, two big, fish-like animals swim right up to the glass, as if to greet them. Jean tells Ricky that these friendly animals are called *dolphins* (DOHL-fins).

One of the dolphins suddenly turns and shoots up toward the surface of the water. Jean and Ricky run outdoors and up to a platform at the edge of the tank, where they can see the dolphin better.

"Look!" laughs Ricky, "The dolphin is coming out of the water to say hello to us!"

The children decide that this friendly character is their favorite of all the sea animals. They learn that the dolphin trainers at Marine Land have named him "Splash."

Splash is a "bottle-nosed" dolphin. His long nose and jaw form a kind of beak, called a *rostrum*. On his forehead is a round bump called a *melon*.

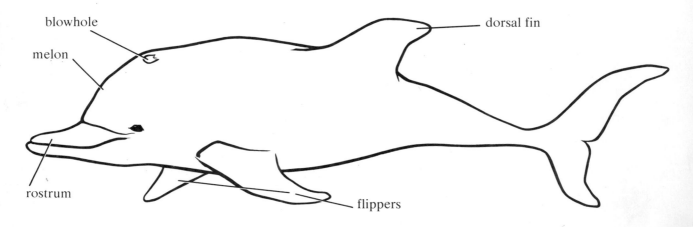

Splash has a long, sleek body. His front flippers and powerful tail help to push him smoothly through the water. Although Splash looks and swims like a fish, he is not a fish at all—he is a mammal, like dogs, horses, cows, and human beings. Like all mammals, he is warm-blooded. He has a thick layer of fat, called *blubber*, that protects his warm body from the cold sea water.

Splash cannot take oxygen from the water as fish can. Like all mammals, he has lungs and must breathe air. So he swims to the surface of the water two or three times a minute and breathes through the blowhole, or air vent, on top of his head.

Dolphins are playful, intelligent animals, and Splash is no exception. He has learned all kinds of games and tricks. One of his favorite tricks is "begging" for food. He comes right out of the water and balances on his tail, ready to grab the fish that Jean holds out for him.

Of course, a little fish like this is just a snack for Splash: he usually eats about 20 pounds (9 kilograms) of fish every day.

After feeding Splash, Jean wants to play another of the dolphin's favorite games—"catch." She tosses a big rubber ball to him, and he tosses it back. But, true to his name, he splashes water all over her. Perhaps he meant to play a joke on Jean; he even looks as though he's smiling at her!

Most dolphins seem to enjoy doing tricks just for the fun of it—they don't have to be given any reward. Sometimes, Splash does tricks all by himself at night, even though he doesn't have an audience.

But when people come to see Splash, he and the other dolphins really put on a show. With the aid of their powerful tails, the dolphins leap high into the air, catching and throwing brightly colored balls. They also do fancy leaps through hoops hung above the water. Altogether, the Marine Land trainers have taught Splash and the other dolphins over 50 different tricks.

One of the dolphins' favorite games is basketball. They seem to have a natural talent for it. In fact, when dolphins swim wild in the ocean they often find floating objects and bounce or balance them on their noses for fun.

Because dolphins are so intelligent and have such a natural desire to play, they can easily be taught to do many tricks in a very short time.

Hugh, a trainer at Marine Land, has taught Splash and another dolphin named Sam to "sing." Of course, they don't really sing. But they do make strange whistling sounds by forcing air through internal passages that lead to the blowholes on their heads. Dolphins normally use these sounds to communicate with each other under water.

When their singing act is over, Splash and Sam take a bow together. They're a big success with the crowd, and everyone applauds.

People love to watch the dolphins' antics, and are amazed that such large animals can leap so high and do so many tricks. The dolphins *are* huge: Splash is eight feet (2.4 meters) long and weighs 400 pounds (180 kilograms). In spite of his size, he is a fast swimmer. On the surface of the water, he can swim at speeds up to 25 mph (40 kmph); under water he swims even faster. By steering with his tail, his flippers, and the fin on his back (called a *dorsal fin*), he can twist and turn easily in any direction. So, although Splash is a large animal, he has no trouble moving quickly through the water.

Splash is finished performing for the day, but he seems to want to play a little longer. He pops out of the water with a friendly grin, right in front of Ricky. At first, Ricky is afraid of Splash. The dolphin has an awful lot of teeth! But Hugh tells Ricky that even wild dolphins are very friendly and have never been known to hurt people.

He says that when sailors are out at sea, they often see groups of friendly dolphins swimming alongside their boats, as if to keep them company. The sailors believe that dolphins bring them luck and good sailing weather. There are also stories of dolphins that have helped to guide ships safely through shallow harbors and dangerous waters. And it is even said that dolphins sometimes rescue people from drowning by pushing them to the safety of the shore.

When he hears these stories, Ricky decides that it will be safe to pet Splash. Splash seems to love it; in fact, he comes right up on the platform for more!

Hugh tells Jean and Ricky that dolphins are especially fond of children. He says that stories handed down to us from ancient Greece and Rome tell of several wild dolphins that made friends with young children. According to the stories, the dolphins actually allowed children to ride through the water on their backs. The ancient sculpture in this picture shows a boy riding a dolphin, just as the stories describe.

Such friendships have been formed in modern times, too. In New Zealand, in the 1950's, a wild dolphin came into the harbor of a town called Opononi. The dolphin played with the children who were swimming there, and it made special friends with a 13-year-old girl. It allowed itself to be petted and stroked, and it even gave the girl rides on its back.

Now that the children know more about dolphins, they are not afraid to play with Splash at all. Jean even learns to "shake hands" with Splash when he jumps out of the water.

Hugh tells the children that dolphins are more than just interesting playmates. He says that scientists are now studying dolphins in order to learn about their special direction-finding systems. The scientists have learned that dolphins do not have a sense of smell, and that although they have good eyesight, they often can't see very well in muddy water. Yet the animals never have trouble finding food. This is because they use a system called *echo-location*.

As they swim through the water, the dolphins give off constant creaking noises—noises that bounce back, or echo, when they strike a solid object such as a fish. By waiting for the echo, dolphins can tell exactly where to find the fish they are looking for. Scientists hope to use their studies of echo-location to develop better navigation systems for ships and submarines.

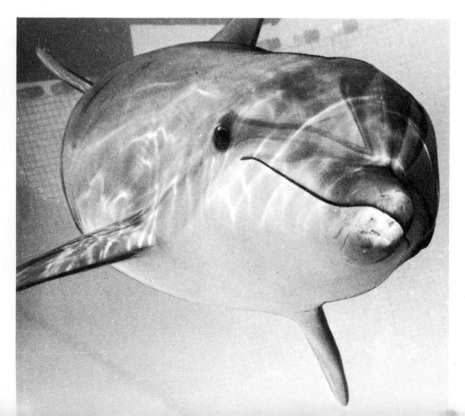

As Jean and Ricky have found out, people can learn a lot from dolphins. These animals are not only intelligent and interesting, but they are very gentle creatures that rarely fight with their neighbors in the sea. They have learned to get along peacefully with each other, with other sea animals, and even with human beings.

DO YOU KNOW . . .

- how many kinds of dolphins there are?

- what makes a dolphin different from a porpoise?

- how dolphins breathe air when they are sleeping?

TO FIND THE ANSWERS TO THESE QUESTIONS,
TURN THE PAGE 👉

FACTS ABOUT DOLPHINS

Although dolphins look much like fish, they are actually mammals, like humans, dogs, or cows. They are warm-blooded, and they breathe air. The mothers nurse their babies under water.

One part of the dolphin's body that looks different from that of a fish is its tail. A dolphin's tail is horizontal in relation to its body, whereas a fish's tail is vertical.

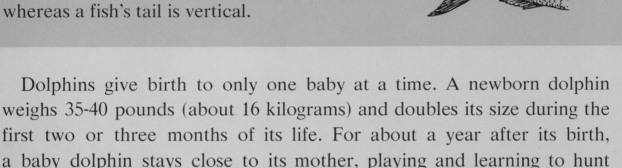

Dolphins give birth to only one baby at a time. A newborn dolphin weighs 35-40 pounds (about 16 kilograms) and doubles its size during the first two or three months of its life. For about a year after its birth, a baby dolphin stays close to its mother, playing and learning to hunt for fish. If the mother should die, another female dolphin will adopt the baby until it is old enough to take care of itself.

People often confuse dolphins with porpoises. This is because dolphins and porpoises look very much alike. But there is a difference between the two. A dolphin has a long snout that forms a sort of "beak," whereas a porpoise has a blunt snout, without a beak.

Porpoise

Dolphin

Since dolphins breathe air, they must come to the water's surface often, even when sleeping. So dolphins sleep by taking little "cat-naps" just below the surface of the water. Every few minutes, the sleeping dolphins surface and breathe without even waking up.

The bottle-nosed dolphin, shown in this book, is one of about 30 kinds of dolphins. These dolphins, as well as porpoises and toothed whales, all belong to the same family. Shown below are a few of the bottle-nose's close relatives.

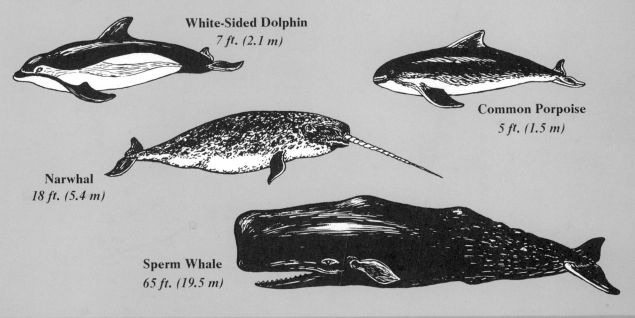

White-Sided Dolphin
7 ft. (2.1 m)

Common Porpoise
5 ft. (1.5 m)

Narwhal
18 ft. (5.4 m)

Sperm Whale
65 ft. (19.5 m)

Dolphins are even more intelligent than dogs. Most scientists compare the dolphin's intelligence to that of the chimpanzee, which is thought to be the animal closest in intelligence to human beings.

The Animal Friends Books

Clover the CALF
Jessie the CHICKEN
Ali the DESERT FOX
Splash the DOLPHIN
Dolly the DONKEY
Downy the DUCKLING
ELEPHANTS around the World
Tippy the FOX TERRIER
Marigold the GOLDFISH
Polly the GUINEA PIG
Winslow the HAMSTER
Figaro the HORSE

Rusty the IRISH SETTER
Boots the KITTEN
Penny and Pete the LAMBS
The LIONS of Africa
Mandy the MONKEY
Lorito the PARROT
Curly the PIGLET
Whiskers the RABBIT
Shelley the SEA GULL
Penelope the TORTOISE
Sprig the TREE FROG
Tanya the TURTLE DOVE

CAROLRHODA BOOKS
241 FIRST AVENUE NORTH — MINNEAPOLIS, MINNESOTA 55401

Published in memory of Carolrhoda Locketz Rozell,
Who loved to bring children and books together

Please write for a complete catalogue

DATE DUE			
SEP 26 '83			
APR 2 '84			
Morris			
SEP 16 '85			
APR 11			
3			
APR 23 '96			
Mohris			
Morris			